HUSH SONGS

AFRICAN AMERICAN LULLABIES

JOYCE CAROL THOMAS

ILLUSTRATIONS BY

BRENDA JOYSMITH

JUMP AT THE SUN

HYPERION BOOKS FOR CHILDREN

NEW YORK

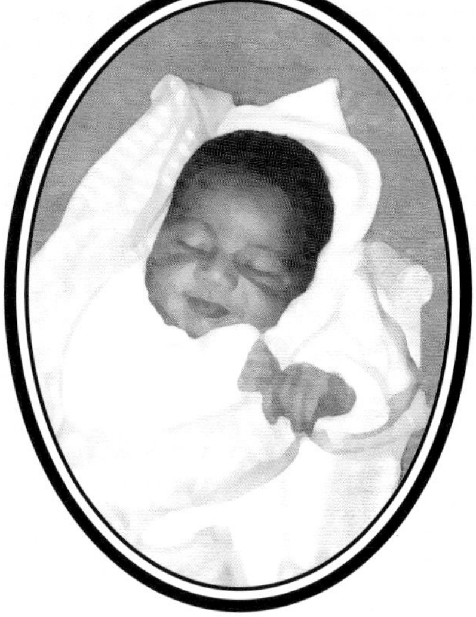

For Michaela Pecot
With love—J.C.T.

For Natalia Anderson
With love—B.J.

For information address Hyperion Books for Children, 114 Fifth Avenue, New York, New York 10011-5690.

Printed in Singapore. First Edition 5 7 9 10 8 6 4
This book is set in 14-pt. Deepdene.
Music set by Media Lynx. Designed by Christine Kettner. Visit www.jumpatthesun.com
LC 00-102748 ISBN 0-7868-0562-5 (trade) ISBN 0-7868-2488-3 (lib. bdg.)

INTRODUCTION

WHAT IS AN AFRICAN AMERICAN HUSH SONG? It is a mother sound, sung by cradling mothers. It is a father sound, sung by caring fathers. It is a comforting sound, dreamy and murmuring from the harp mouths of mothers, rolling deep and abiding from the drum mouths of fathers. An African American hush song is a reflection of an ancient memory, as ancient as the throbbing cadences of African drums. An African American hush song is a lull as quieting as the meditating rivers that whisper along the beautiful American landscape. A forward-moving rhythm. As forward-moving as tomorrow's promise for today's child. A hush song is a traditional lullaby, such as "All the Pretty Little Horses," or an inspirational gospel song such as "Somebody Bigger Than You and I," sung softly.

Historically, African American women rocked the children in their charge with the lullabies imported from Europe. But in the singing, this new woman, this African American woman, made the melodies her own, embellished them with African meaning. As with so much that we heard as we arrived on these shores, we took the sounds and shaped them new. With these songs, we did just as we had done with everything we found here in the New World: we created something beyond what we had received. And in our unique way we wove deeper tones, richer rhythms, and more immediate language. Then we crooned these songs to our own babies, echoing joy back out into the world, for we are an immensely creative people.

When my seventh granddaughter was born, I started thinking about the songs I would croon to her. I hope that a rich variety of those songs is reflected here. Some of the older lullabies are Anglo-Saxon music transfigured into African American music. They reflect the vitality of our culture, and can be heard on any day interpreted by notable vocalists, including legendary singers such as Marian Anderson and Mahalia Jackson. The contemporary hush songs included here underline the subtle truth of the collection: that African Americans created then and we continue to create now. Harry Belafonte, Marion Williams, and Oscar Brown, Jr., have presented these contemporary songs. Steven Roberts, the internationally famous gospel composer, collaborated with me on "A Song for You," presented for the first time in this collection. Olly Wilson, a gifted consultant, composer, musicologist, professor of music, and grandfather, composed the melody to my lyrics for "The Angels' Lullaby." While the hush songs here are notated as melodies with chord changes in simple, easy-to-read notations, it's important to remember that improvisation was and is a vital part of the African American musical tradition. I hope that parents, children, and teachers will, from time to time, liberate themselves from the confines of the written notes and let their voices carry these songs beyond their basic boundaries.

More than anything else, hush songs are musical heralds of peace, moving free as air across time, space, and cultural borders. All people—yesterday, today, and tomorrow—have sung, now sing, and will sing hush songs to all our children and babies. For a child, a parent's love is the most important emotion in the world. A generous lap, the most important place in the world. A heartfelt hug, the most important touch in the world. A soul-shaped song, the most important sound in the world. May it ever be so.

—Joyce Carol Thomas

CONTENTS

All the Pretty Little Horses

Recognized as a traditional African American lullaby, "All the Pretty Little Horses" has been sung by artists as diverse in style as Odetta and Judy Collins. This all-time favorite has been arranged by a host of composers, and can be heard many a night soothing a child to sleep, with each verse ending with the lulling "all the pretty little horses."

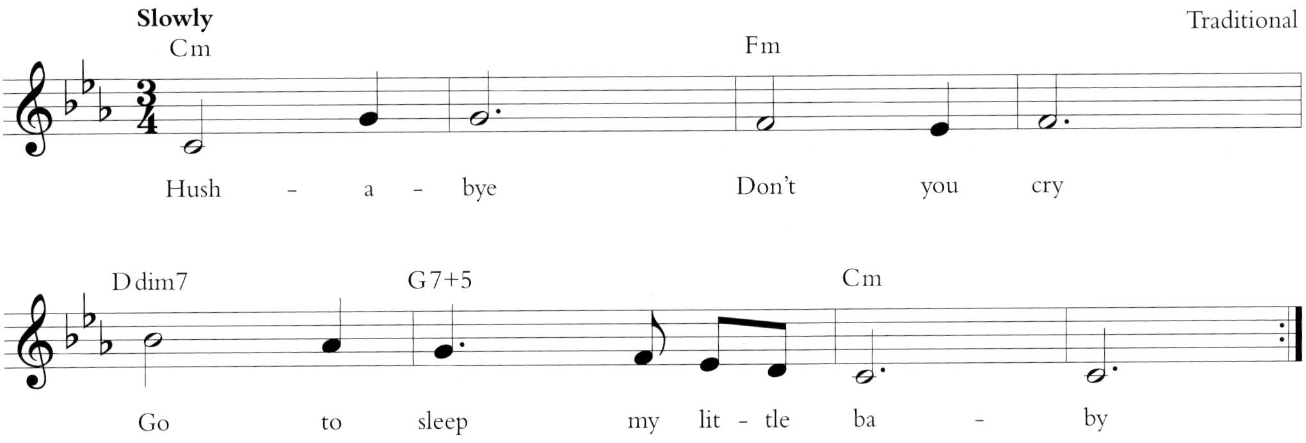
Slowly
Traditional
Cm
Fm
Hush - a - bye
Don't you cry
Ddim7
G7+5
Cm
Go to sleep my lit - tle ba - by

When you wake
You shall have
All the pretty little horses

Blacks and bays
Dapples and grays
All the pretty little horses

Hush-a-bye
Don't you cry
Go to sleep
My little baby

When you wake
You shall have
All the pretty little horses

The Angels' Lullaby

The 1999 "Angels' Lullaby," with its rocking-chair-ready sway, was composed by Olly Wilson. With lyrics by Joyce Carol Thomas it celebrates the birth in 1998 of Ms. Thomas's seventh granddaughter, Michaela Pecot. In addition, it is dedicated to Olly Wilson's first granddaughter, Taylor Grace Johnson, who was born in 1995. The pride of grandparents is reflected in the music and text, delicately embodied in the restful melody and the endearing lyrics.

Lyrics by Joyce Carol Thomas
Music by Olly Wilson

THE ANGELS' LULLABY

time to say good night, The moon is on the rise And
choir of heav'n - ly an - gels Kiss-ing your sleep - y face
when you're sound a - sleep Soft-ly a - way they'll fly Through
se - ven an - gels fly down with star - light in their eyes
Gath-er - ing 'round your bed - side with wings of shin - ing grace
moon - beams and star - light home to sky on high
Se - ven an - gels sing - ing bed - time lul - la - bies

of hob - by horse dreams and ted - dy bears and hap - py hugs and
mf
rock - ing chairs
1., 2.
2. A
3. And
mf
mp

3.
3.
p
Dolce
pp
ppp
let fade away

Brown Baby

"Brown Baby" was written by Oscar Brown, Jr., and published during the 1960s Civil Rights period. This hush song is highly regarded by children in many countries. The beautiful words are a singing prayer, an incantation, of the hopes and aspirations that African American parents hold for their children.

Lyrics and Music by Oscar Brown, Jr.

Slowly, with feeling
E♭m A♭m9 Fdim B♭7
Brown___ Ba - by, Brown Ba - by, as you grow___ up I
Ba - by, Brown Ba-by, as years roll by I want you
E♭m A♭m9 Fm7 B♭7
want you to drink from the plen - ty cup I
to go with your head held high I want you
E♭m A♭m7 Fm7 B♭7+5
want you to stand up tall and___ proud I
to live by the justice code I want you to
E♭m A♭m9 Fdim
want you to speak up___ clear and
walk down the free - dom___ free - dom

1.
B♭7 E♭m E♭m
loud Brown Ba - by Brown
2.
B♭7 E♭m E♭m
road Brown Ba - by Now
A♭m7 E♭m E♭m
Lie a - way, lie a - way sleep - ing
A♭m7 B♭7 E♭m
Lie a - way here in my arms while your
A♭m7 B♭7 E♭m
dad - dy and ma - ma pro - tect you and
G♭m A♭m7
keep you safe from harm oh you lit - tle Brown

BROWN BABY

E♭m A♭m9 Fdim B♭7
Ba - by Brown Ba - by, it makes me glad that
E♭m A♭m9 Fm7 B♭7
you will have things I have nev - er had. When
E♭m A♭m9 Fdim B♭7+5 E♭m
out of men's hearts all the hate is hurled you're going to
A♭m7 B♭7
live in a bet - ter world
E♭m
Brown Ba - by

He's Got the Whole World in His Hands

"He's Got the Whole World in His Hands," in its democratic view of the world, retains the essence of the very soul of African America. This traditional spiritual takes on the aspects of a hush song when its soothing power is presented in heavenly voice. The soulful melody can be delivered to tiny ears when quiet time is needed or when night stars cover the sleepy-time skies.

Traditional
Medium-fast tempo
A♭
He's got the whole world in His hands, He's got the
E♭7
A♭
big round world in His hands, He's got the whole world
A♭/E♭
E♭7
A♭
in His hands, He's got the whole world in His hands He's got

He's got my brothers and sisters in His hands
He's got my brothers and sisters in His hands
He's got my brothers and sisters in His hands
He's got the whole world in His hands

He's got the sun and the rain in His hands
He's got the sun and the rain in His hands
He's got the sun and the rain in His hands
He's got the whole world in His hands

He's got rivers and the mountains in His hands
He's got rivers and the mountains in His hands
He's got rivers and the mountains in His hands
He's got the whole world in His hands

He's got everybody here in His hands
He's got everybody here in His hands
He's got everybody here in His hands
He's got the whole world in His hands

The Lord's Prayer

"The Lord's Prayer" is a found hush song with a text taken directly from the King James edition of the Bible. Its slow, expressive melodic line is the perfect hush song when sung softly. This Albert Hay Mallotte arrangement can be heard interpreted by Mahalia Jackson, who is regarded by many as the "World's Greatest Gospel Singer." Presented in a multitude of African American churches to express an abiding faith, it is also used at home to settle children down to sleep.

Arrangement by Albert Hay Mallotte

Rubato—slowly, with feeling

A E7/G♯ A Bm7 E7
Our Fa - ther Which art in hea - ven
F♯m7 Bm7 E7 A A/G♯ F♯m7 G♯7
Hall - o - wed be Thy name Thy king - dom
C♯m F♯m7 C♯7/G♯ F♯m7/A C♯7
come Thy will be done on
F♯m7 D A Bm7 E7 A
earth as it is in hea - ven

THE LORD'S PRAYER

Bm7/F♯ Am/E Bm/D A/C♯ F♯m Bm7 E7 A
Give us this day our dai - ly bread And for -
F♯m G♯M F♯m/G♯ G♯7
give us our debts as we for - give our debt - ors
G♯ A Bm
and lead us not in - to temp - ta - tion but de -
BM7 EM7 A C♯ A
li - ver us from e - vil for thine is the
DM7 Bm7/D BM7/D♯ Edim7
king - dom and the pow - er and the glo - ry for
A/E F♯/E E7 A/E A/E Bm7 E7 A D A
ev - - - er A men

Raisins and Almonds

The very calming "Raisins and Almonds" is an appealing, traditional hush song, treasured by African American children. It can be harmonized in the bonding voice of communal assurance or it can be a solo crooned with the intimacy of a mother's sweet promise. The gentle, repetitive exhortation to sleep at the end of the song urges a listening child along the path to slumber.

Traditional

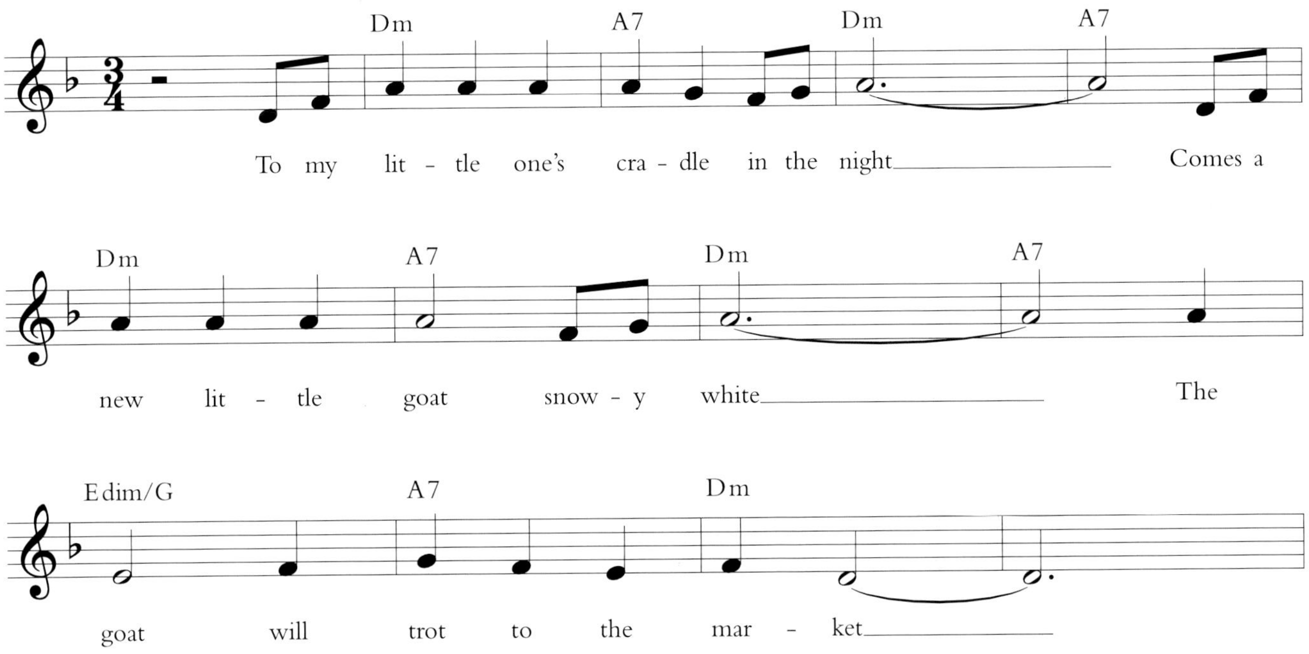
Dm A7 Dm A7
To my lit - tle one's cra - dle in the night Comes a
Dm A7 Dm A7
new lit - tle goat snow - y white The
Edim/G A7 Dm
goat will trot to the mar - ket

RAISINS AND ALMONDS

Gm/B♭ Gm A7
While mo - ther her watch will keep To
Emin/G A7 Dm
bring you back rais - ins and al - monds
A7 A7 Dm
Sleep, my lit - tle one, Sleep To
Emin/G A7 Dm
bring you back rais - ins and al - monds
A7 A7 Dm
Sleep, my lit - tle one, Sleep
A7 A7 Dm
Sleep, my lit - tle one, Sleep

Petal Child

Poetic in its power, this 1975 composition by Joyce Carol Thomas is an anthem of peace for all children. The song about an imaginary toddler has the remarkable ability to make each child feel loved. "Petal Child" evokes the renewing promise of spring and creates the aura of a hush song, tender and sleepy-time soft.

Lyrics and Music by Joyce Carol Thomas

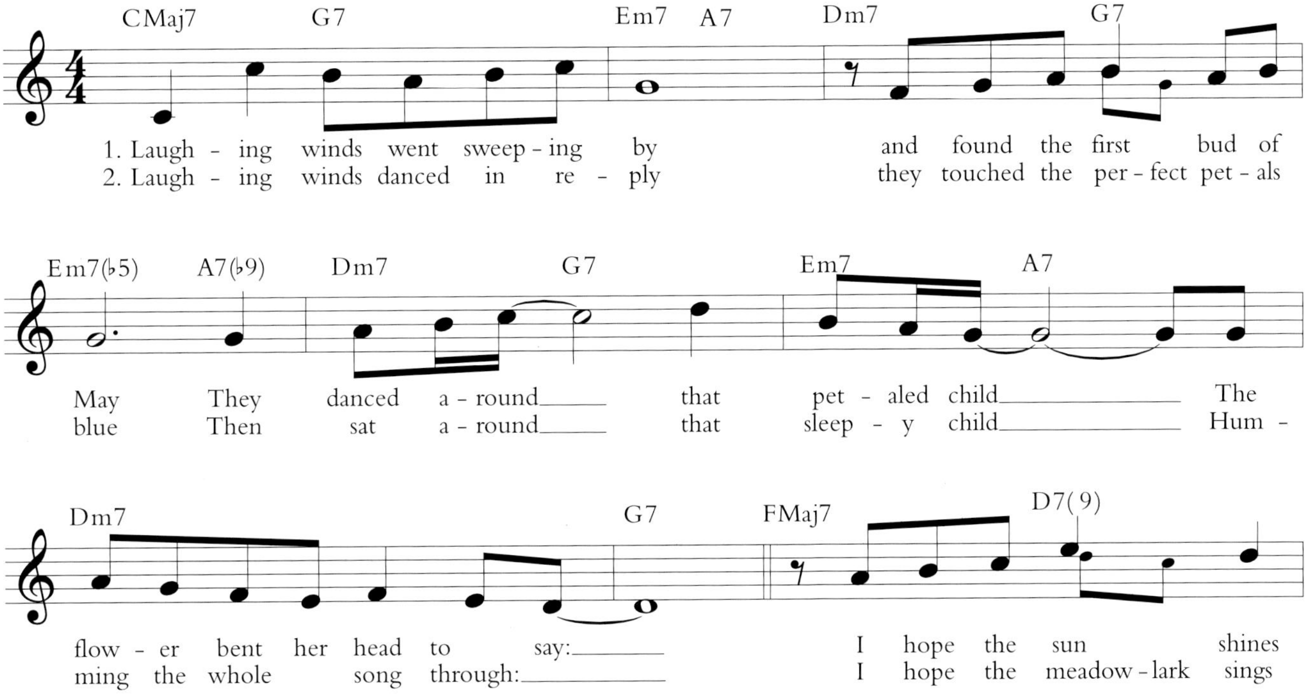

CMaj7 G7 Em7 A7 Dm7 G7
1. Laugh - ing winds went sweep - ing by and found the first bud of
2. Laugh - ing winds danced in re - ply they touched the per - fect pet - als
Em7(♭5) A7(♭9) Dm7 G7 Em7 A7
May They danced a - round that pet - aled child The
blue Then sat a - round that sleep - y child Hum -
Dm7 G7 FMaj7 D7(9)
flow - er bent her head to say: I hope the sun shines
ming the whole song through: I hope the meadow - lark sings

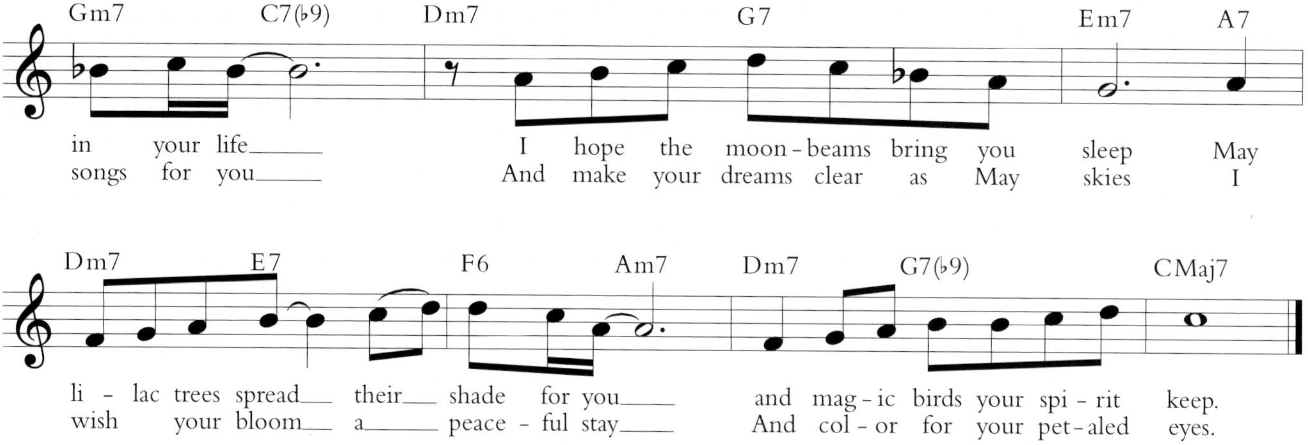
Gm7 C7(♭9) Dm7 G7 Em7 A7
in your life___ I hope the moon-beams bring you sleep May
songs for you___ And make your dreams clear as May skies I
Dm7 E7 F6 Am7 Dm7 G7(♭9) CMaj7
li - lac trees spread___ their___ shade for you___ and mag-ic birds your spi-rit keep.
wish your bloom___ a___ peace-ful stay___ And col-or for your pet-aled eyes.

Scarlet Ribbons

"Scarlet Ribbons" is a bedtime story told in song. Published in 1952 by the Jack Segal and Evelyn Danzig songwriting team, it is well cherished by African American children. Its simple, easily hummed notes and lyrics are delivered to children when the sandman is near. Harry Belafonte's touching version is particularly striking.

Slowly

Lyrics and Music by Jack Segal and Evelyn Danzig

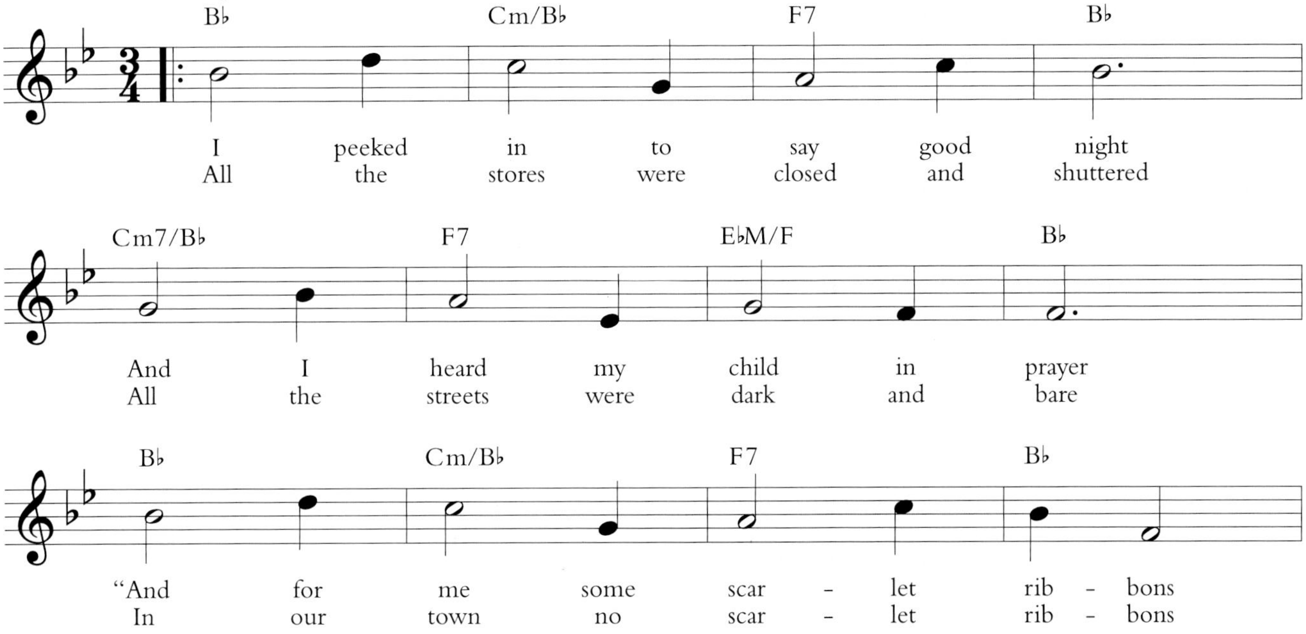

B♭ Cm/B♭ F7 B♭
I peeked in to say good night
All the stores were closed and shuttered
Cm7/B♭ F7 E♭M/F B♭
And I heard my child in prayer
All the streets were dark and bare
B♭ Cm/B♭ F7 B♭
"And for me some scar - let rib - bons
In our town no scar - let rib - bons

SCARLET RIBBONS

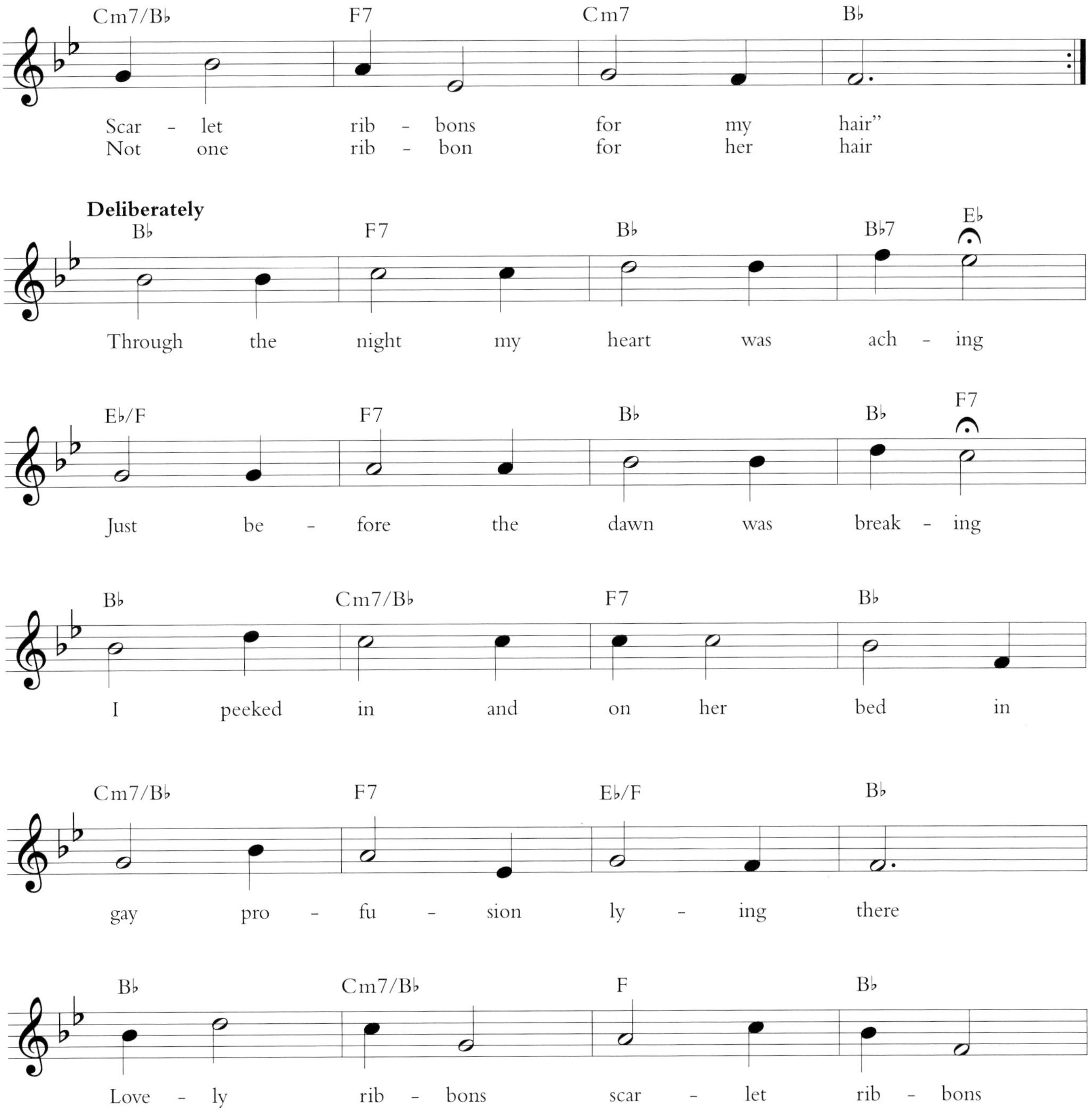
Cm7/B♭ F7 Cm7 B♭
Scar - let rib - bons for my hair"
Not one rib - bon for her hair
Deliberately
B♭ F7 B♭ B♭7 E♭
Through the night my heart was ach - ing
E♭/F F7 B♭ B♭ F7
Just be - fore the dawn was break - ing
B♭ Cm7/B♭ F7 B♭
I peeked in and on her bed in
Cm7/B♭ F7 E♭/F B♭
gay pro - fu - sion ly - ing there
B♭ Cm7/B♭ F B♭
Love - ly rib - bons scar - let rib - bons

SCARLET RIBBONS

Cm7/B♭ F7 E♭/F B♭
scar - let rib - bons for her hair
B♭ F7 B♭ B♭7 E♭
If I live to be a hun - dred
E♭/F F7 B♭ B♭ F7
I will nev - er know from where
B♭ Cm/B♭ F B♭
Came those love - ly scar - let rib - bons
Cm7/B♭ F7 E♭/F FMaj7 B♭
Scar - let rib - bons for her hair

Somebody Bigger Than You and I

"Somebody Bigger Than You and I" is at once an expression of wonder at the creation of the world in all its natural splendors and simultaneously a statement of profound religious conviction. This inspirational offering, colored in the vernacular, reflects the personal belief in a higher power, in "somebody bigger than you and I." "Somebody Bigger Than You and I" has become a means of transmitting traditional faith to children.

Lyrics and Music by J. Lange, H. Heath, and S. Burke

GM
Em9
Who___ made the moun-tains___ Who___ made the trees___
Bm
Em
Am7
D7
Who___ made the ri - vers___ Flow out___ to the seas___
G
Am7
G/B
CM
C♯dim7
Who___ hung the moon___ In the star - ry sky
G/D
G
Am
G/B
Am
Am
D7
G
Some-bo - dy big - ger than you___ and I___

SOMEBODY BIGGER THAN YOU AND I

GM Em9
Who made the flow-ers To bloom in the spring? Tell me who
Bm Em Am7 D7
writes the song For the lit-tle ro-bin to sing? And
G Am7 G/B CM C♯dim7
who sends the rain When the air seems dry?
G/D G Am G/B Am Am D7 GM
Some-bo-dy big-ger than you and I You know who,
Am7 D7 GM Am7 GM/G B7(♯5)
God He lights my way When my road gets dark
Em7 D7 GM A♯dim7 Bm
keeps me God keeps me com-pan-y with His love to guide you the
Bm Em A7 D C♯dim/E D/F♯ D7
Lord He walks right be-side you just like he walks with me

SOMEBODY BIGGER THAN YOU AND I

GM Em7
When I get so lone-ly Ma-ny times I'm filled with des-pair and
Bm7 Em Am7 D
Who gives me cou-rage just to Go on from there and
G Am7 G/B G CM BM7 Em A7/C♯
who gives me faith that will ne-ver ne-ver die
GM/D Am7/D GM/D Am/D GM/D Am7/D GM/D Am7/D
Some-bo-dy big-ger Some-bo-dy big-ger than
Am7 D7 G
you than you and I

A Song for You

In 1985 Steven Roberts composed gospel music to Joyce Carol Thomas's lyrics for "A Song for You," which was dedicated to Ms. Thomas's firstborn granddaughter, Aresa Pecot. The simple melody, with the characteristic rhythmic nuances of gospel, captures the idea of creation, which is suggested by the song's text and evokes a fascinating sound-poem for children.

Lyrics by Joyce Carol Thomas
Music by Joyce Carol Thomas and Steven Roberts

Intro
G♭ A♭ B♭ A♭ G♭ B♭
B♭Maj7 A♭Maj7
Let me make a song for you
B♭Maj7 A♭Maj7
Let me make a song for you
G♭Maj7 A♭Maj7 B♭Maj7 A♭Maj7 G♭Maj7 B♭Maj7
How will I be - gin? How will I be - gin?

A SONG FOR YOU

A-7 D7(♭9) B-7 E-7 C B-7 E-
Think I'll bor-row a note from a swal-low's throat
C D C D E
and co-lor it with vi-o-lins and co-lor it with vi-o-lins
Interlude
F7(♭5) EMaj7 F7(♭5) EMaj7
and co-lor it with vi-o-lins
F♯-7 G♯-7 F♯-7
Let me make a song for you let me see
EMaj7 A-7 D7 B-7 E-7
where it goes I think to a place
CMaj7 B-7 E-
where the clar-in-ets race
C D E C D
and a strum-ming gui-tar slows and a strum-ming gui-tar

E
F7(♭5)
EMaj7
slows and a strum - ming gui - tar slows
Interlude
F7(♭5)
EMaj7
2
2
𝄋
D♭
F-7/C
D♭-7
G♭7(9)
AMaj7
BMaj7
D♭
Let me make a song for you how will it end?
G♭
F-7
B♭-
G♭
A♭
In the soft sud - den rite of a sax - o - phone
B♭-
G♭
A♭
B♭
night and the rhy - ming of the wind
G♭
A♭
B♭
and the rhy - ming of the wind
Interlude
D.S. al Coda
BMaj7
A♭7
BMaj7
D♭Maj7
E♭Maj7
BMaj7
D♭Maj7
E♭Maj7
vamp to fade